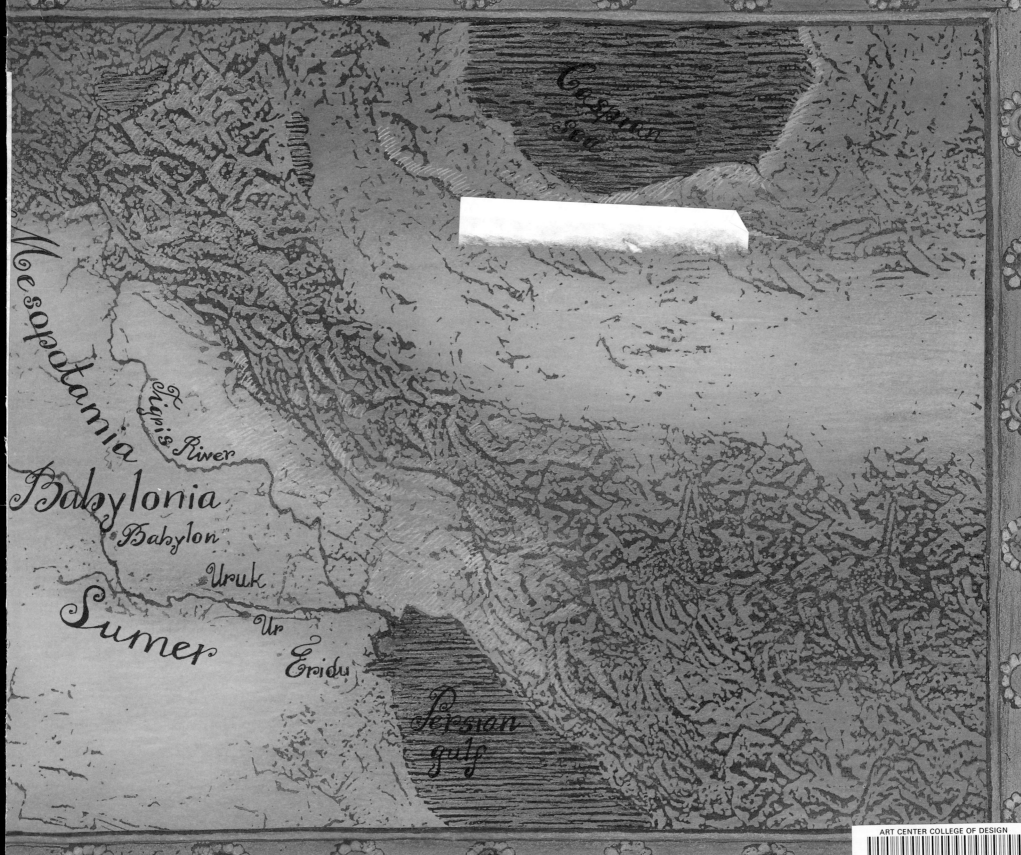

Caspian Sea

Mesopotamia

Tigris River

Babylonia

Babylon

Uruk

Sumer

Ur

Eridu

Persian gulf

LONG AGO in the land of Mesopotamia,
a king by the name of Gilgamesh
was sent by the Sun God to rule over
the city of Uruk.

Gilgamesh was part god and part man.
He looked human, but he did not know what
it was to be human. He had power and wealth
but he was not happy. He had everything
except friends. He was always alone.
Because of this he grew bitter and cruel.

One day, he decided to show
how strong and powerful he was
and make the people remember him forever.

S O IT WAS that Gilgamesh ordered a great wall to be built around the city. He ordered the men to leave their jobs and families to work on it. He made the women bring food. Children were kept away so no one would stop to play with them. At first, the people helped willingly. Their king must have good reason for wanting the wall. Was an enemy planning to attack the city?

B<small>UT AS THE WALL</small> got higher and higher, the people grew restless. How high did it have to be?
It went up higher than any wall in the world, but Gilgamesh pushed on day and night.
Men fainted from work and hunger. Food grew scarce. The people cried out for mercy,
begging Gilgamesh to stop but he would not listen. In despair, they prayed to the Sun God for help.

THE SUN GOD heard their prayers and ordered the creation of another man as strong as Gilgamesh. His name was Enkidu. He was made from the clay of the earth.
Since Gilgamesh had learned nothing from living with people, Enkidu was sent to live with the animals of the forest. As he got to know the animals, he learned to care for them. But he did not know human kindness for he had never seen another person.

THE FIRST MAN Enkidu saw he did not like. It was a hunter chasing animals through the forest, trying to kill them. Why would anyone want to do that? Enkidu wondered.

He rushed to help his friends. He threw the hunter from his chariot and rescued the wounded animals.

The hunter ran back to Uruk to warn Gilgamesh about the new danger in the forest.

He called Enkidu "the strongest man in the world."

GILGAMESH WAS FURIOUS. "There is no one as strong as I am," he said.
"Bring this creature to me so I can prove it. I will destroy him in front of all the people of Uruk."
The hunter said that he could not capture so strong a wild man by himself.
"Then," said Gilgamesh, "we will trick him into coming. Take the singer Shamhat.
Let her lure him here with her songs and charms."

I T WAS SAID that the only person in Uruk who did not love Shamhat was Gilgamesh
and that was because he loved no one. She was the most beautiful woman in the city
and the finest singer in the temple. But could she tame the wild man?
The hunter did not want to return to the forest to be made a fool of again,
but he dared not argue with Gilgamesh, or disobey him.

THE HUNTER LED Shamhat to the place in the forest where he had last seen Enkidu. He left her alone and fled back to the city. As night fell, Shamhat played her harp and sang in the darkness. Her voice cast a spell over the forest. Enkidu walked toward the sound then stopped behind a tree. He had never seen anything so lovely. He approached her slowly so as not to frighten her.

S HAMHAT SAW ENKIDU and stopped singing. He looked more like a beast than a man
but she knew he would not harm her. No one had ever looked at her with so much tenderness.
In the days that followed, Shamhat taught him to speak and to sing and she fell in love with him.
They explored the ways of love together and Enkidu promised he would stay with her always.

SHAMHAT WAS FRIGHTENED. Enkidu must not go near the city of Uruk where Gilgamesh was waiting to destroy him. But Enkidu refused to listen. He was not afraid. He would fight to the death for her.

T HE SADDEST MOMENT for Enkidu was leaving his animal friends. They gathered to watch him go. They could not understand why he was abandoning them and he could not explain.

EACH DAY FROM MORNING until dusk Gilgamesh watched from his tower on top of the great wall of Uruk waiting for Shamhat to return. Everyone in the city had heard of the wild man who might come from the forest and save them from their cruel king. Gilgamesh knew what they were thinking.
He would kill the stranger in front of all the people of Uruk so no one would think of challenging his rule.

SHAMHAT WAS WORRIED. Could Enkidu defeat Gilgamesh? What would people think of this wild creature? To make him look more like other men, she cut his hair and tore part of her robe to cover him. But Enkidu kept his horned crown in memory of his animal friends. Shamhat pointed to Uruk in the distance. Enkidu was dazzled. He had not imagined how beautiful a city could be.

THE NEXT MORNING the people gathered to watch as Shamhat and Enkidu approached the gate.
Gilgamesh had ordered work on the wall stopped for the day so all could see his victory.
He stood on top of the wall and shouted at Enkidu, "I am master of this city and its people!
No one enters without my permission! I dare you to come up here and fight me!"
Enkidu climbed the wall. "I am ready!" he shouted back.

IT WAS THE MOST frightening battle the people of Uruk had ever seen. They fought for hours. The earth shook and lightning flashed across the sky, as if the gods themselves were fighting for control of the world. Gilgamesh and Enkidu were equal in strength and neither was winning. Then, suddenly, Gilgamesh stepped on a loose stone, stumbled and fell over the edge of the wall.

I T HAPPENED SO QUICKLY the people watching could not believe their eyes. To their amazement, Enkidu reached over the wall, grabbed Gilgamesh by the arm and raised him to safety. Why? Enkidu had won. Why would he save someone who was trying to kill him?

GILGAMESH AGAIN STOOD on top of the wall facing Enkidu. All who watched held their breath.
Gilgamesh took a step towards Enkidu, stopped, opened his arms and embraced him.
The king finally understood what it was to be human. He was no longer alone. He had found a friend.

T HE CELEBRATIONS went on for days.
Shamhat was chosen to lead the biggest parade that had ever taken place in Uruk.
Gilgamesh and Enkidu, now brothers, watched and waved from atop the great wall.

GILGAMESH ORDERED work on the wall stopped forever.
Fathers and mothers were reunited and danced with their children in the streets.
Gilgamesh invited everyone to a great feast.

A NEW PEACE settled over Uruk.
On quiet evenings Shamhat liked to go
out on the river with Enkidu and listen
while he and Gilgamesh planned how
they might make the city a happier place.
Then she would play her harp and sing for them,
proud that she had brought them together.
As her voice floated across the water,
the people of Uruk paused to listen.
And they were grateful.

The story of the god-man Gilgamesh is one of the oldest stories in the world; it was inscribed onto clay tablets over 5000 years ago in Mesopotamia (where Iraq and Syria are today). There are many versions of the story but the first people who told it were called Sumerians and Gilgamesh was once their king. The people who lived in Mesopotamia discovered many things: irrigation, the wheel, the first codes of law, the 60-minute hour, and, most important, writing. Without writing the epic of Gilgamesh would certainly have been lost. The Sumerians, and later other Mesopotamians such as the Akkadians, Babylonians and Assyrians, wrote the story in cuneiform, the first script in the world.

Mesopotamia means "the land between the rivers." On a map, one can see two rivers in Iraq: the Tigris and Euphrates. In between these rivers the land was very fertile and allowed for farming. When the ancient peoples started farming these lands over 8000 years ago, the extra food they produced eventually allowed others to build towns and then cities with names like Nippur, Ur, Lagash and Uruk — the setting for the epic of Gilgamesh. The cities became the world's first civilization. Today, because the rivers have changed their course, the land around Uruk is almost entirely a desert, making it hard to believe that it was once covered with farmers' fields, trees and great cities. One can still see the ruins of the wall built by Gilgamesh and the remains of other ancient cities.

Over time other peoples in Mesopotamia told versions of the Gilgamesh legend in places like Akkad, Babylonia and Assyria. Later, parts of the story would make their way into the myths of Egypt, Greece, Persia and even of the Celts in what are now the British Isles. Some of the stories in the Old Testament are said to share similar origins to the epic of Gilgamesh. Mesopotamia is believed to be the setting for the Garden of Eden and the birthplace of Abraham.

Clay tablets were first found in the earth of Iraq and Syria by French and British archeologists in the 19th century. They brought the tablets home with them, and others translated the cuneiform writing later in the century. Today these tablets continue to be found and can be seen in many museums but those containing the Gilgamesh story are rare. The collections in London, Paris and Philadelphia are especially famous.

"For an artist there is no more serious and, at the same time, more joyous task than to create, through art, a new aesthetic, and ultimately, a new way of being."

— *Karel Zeman*

© 1992 Ludmila Zeman

William Heinemann Limited
Michelin House
81 Fulham Road
London SW3 6RB

LONDON   MELBOURNE   AUCKLAND

First published in Great Britain 1992
Originally published in Canada and the United States by Tundra Books, Montreal

ISBN 0 434 96368 2

The artist wishes to thank Dr. T. Cuyler Young, Jr., Director Emeritus and Curator, West Asian Department, Royal Ontario Museum, Toronto; and Dr. Irving Finkel, Assistant Keeper, Department of Western Asiatic Antiquities, The British Museum, London, for their kind assistance.

Design by Dan O'Leary

Printed in Hong Kong by South China Printing Co. Ltd.